T0182611

Copyright © 2011 by Paul Thurlby

All rights reserved. No part of this book may be reproduced, transmitted,
or stored in an information retrieval system in any form or by any means,
graphic, electronic, or mechanical, including photocopying, taping, and
recording, without prior written permission from the publisher.

First U.S. edition 2011

Library of Congress Cataloging-in-Publication Data is available.
Library of Congress Catalog Card Number 2010045400
ISBN 978-0-7636-5565-5

TLF 16 15 14 13 12 11
10 9 8 7 6 5 4 3 2 1

Printed in Dongguan, Guangdong, China

This book was typeset in Delargo DT Infant.
The illustrations were done in digital media.

TEMPLAR BOOKS

an imprint of Candlewick Press
99 Dover Street
Somerville, Massachusetts 02144
www.candlewick.com

PAUL THURLBY'S ALPHABET

Paul thurlby

templar books
an imprint of Candlewick Press

Aa

for

AWESOME!

Bb

B for BOUNCE

C

for

catch

Dd

for

DOG

Ee

for **Embrace**

Ff

BARBICAN

Gg

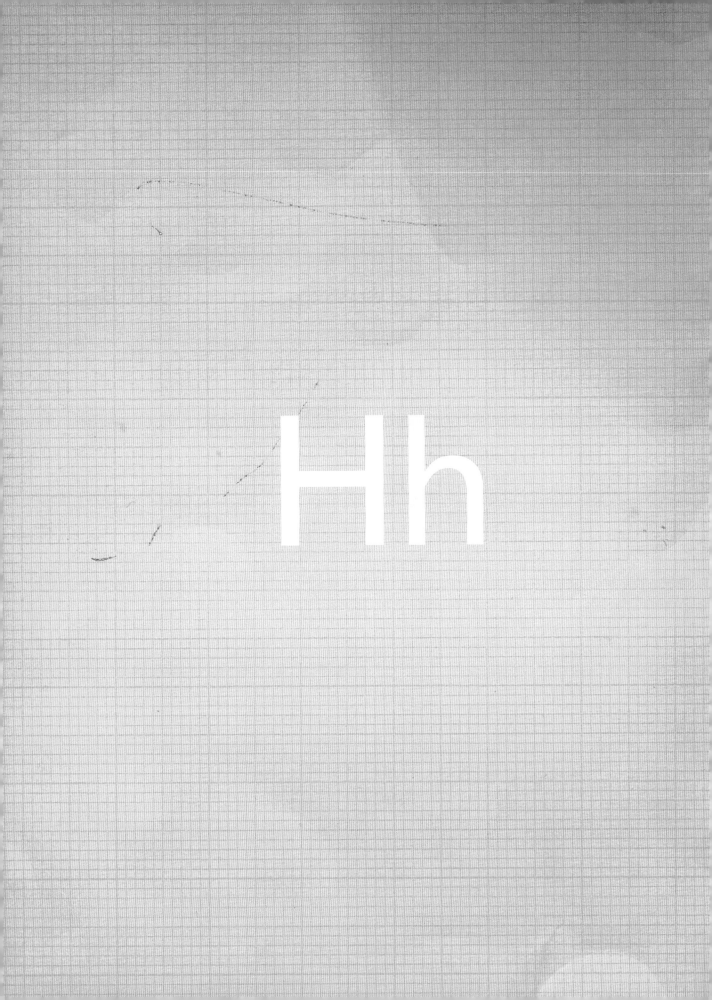

for

HANG

li

Jj

for

JAZZ

Kk

for

KARATE

Ll

for

LIGHTS

Mm

for

MOUNTAIN

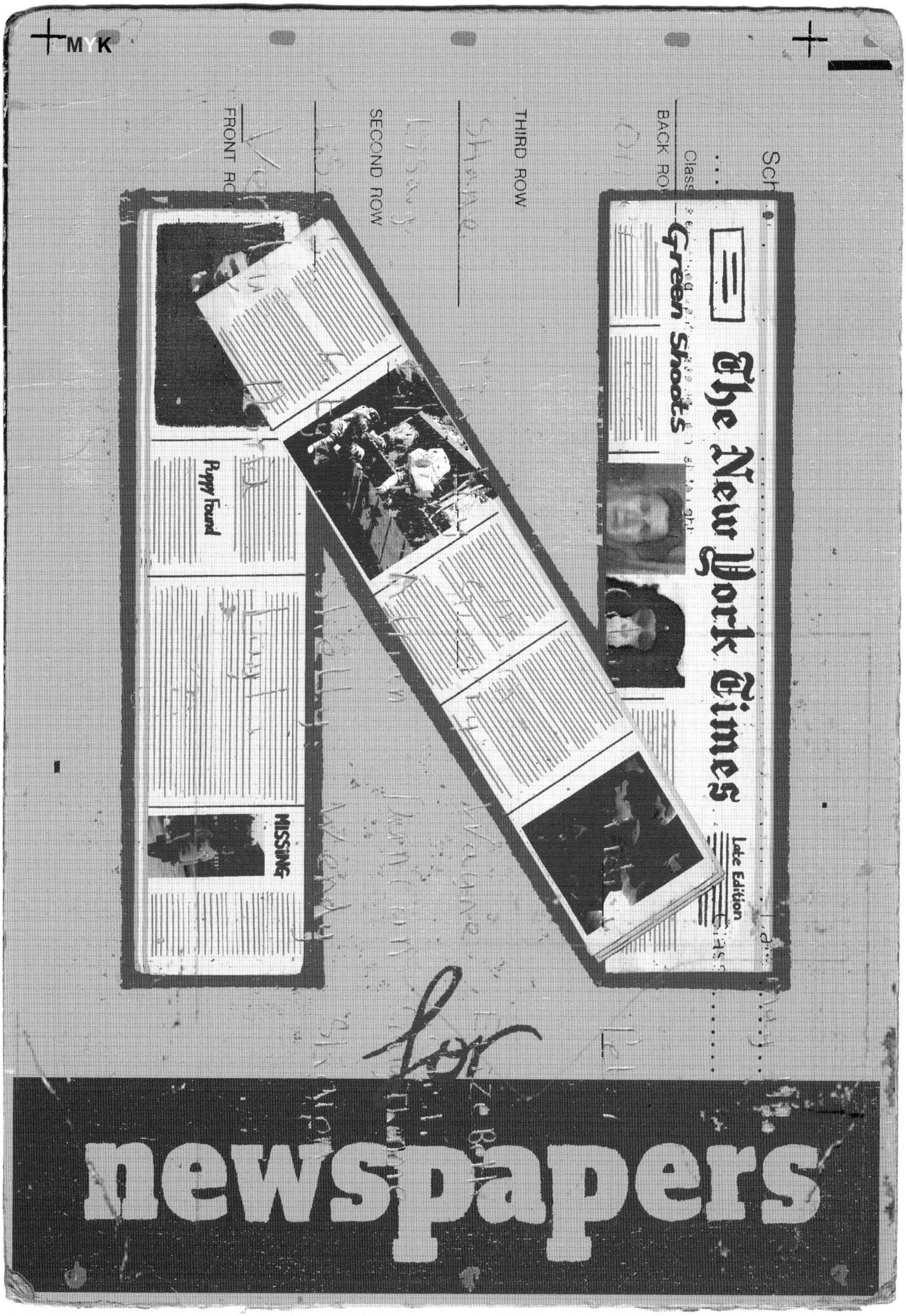

THIRD ROW

SECOND ROW

FRONT RO

BACK RO

Classi

Sch

The New York Times

Green Shoots

Late Edition

Puppy Found

MISSING

for

newspapers

Oo

Pp

for

Pretty

Qq

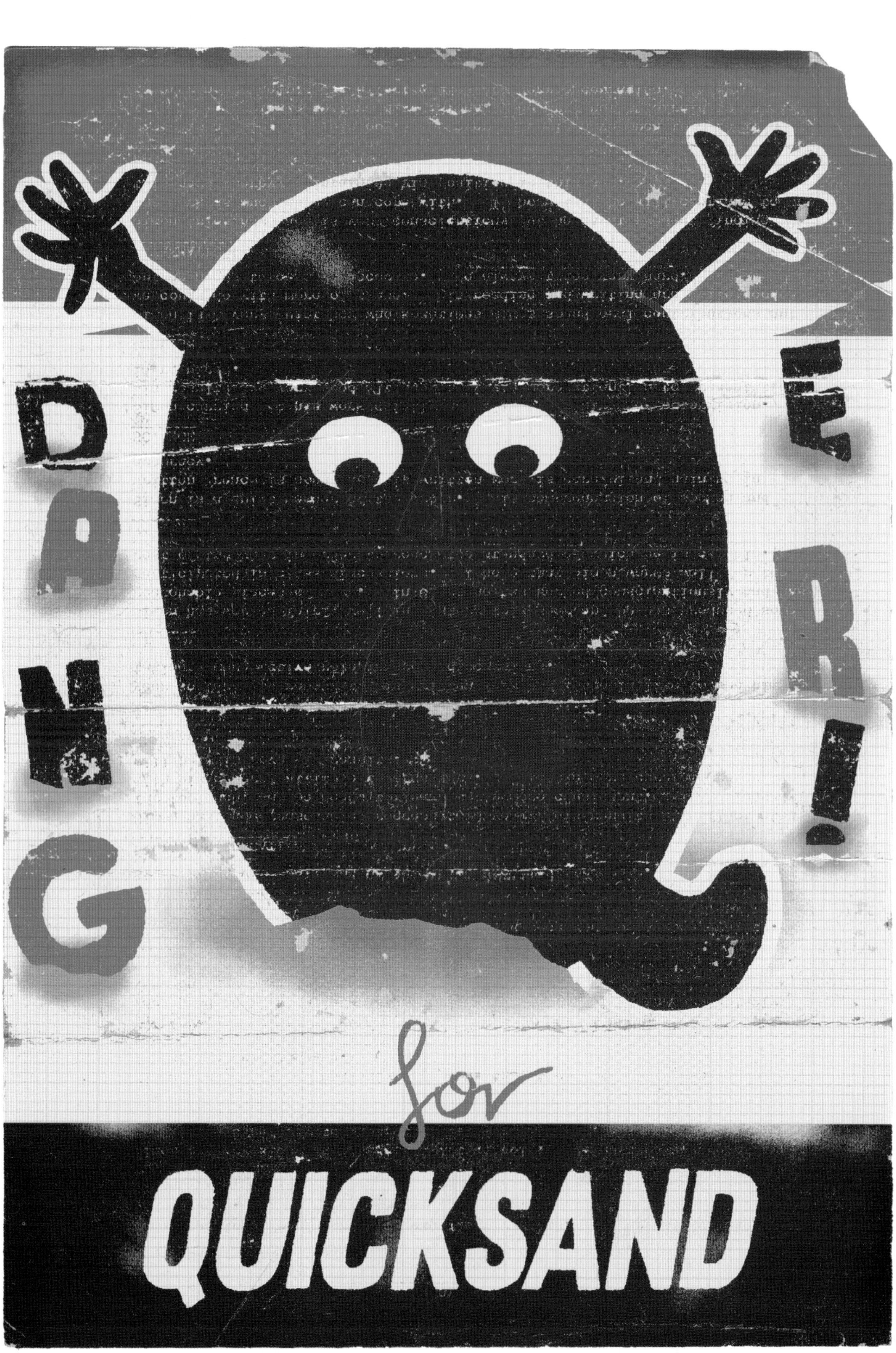
DANGER!
for
QUICKSAND

Rr

for

Rabbit

Ss

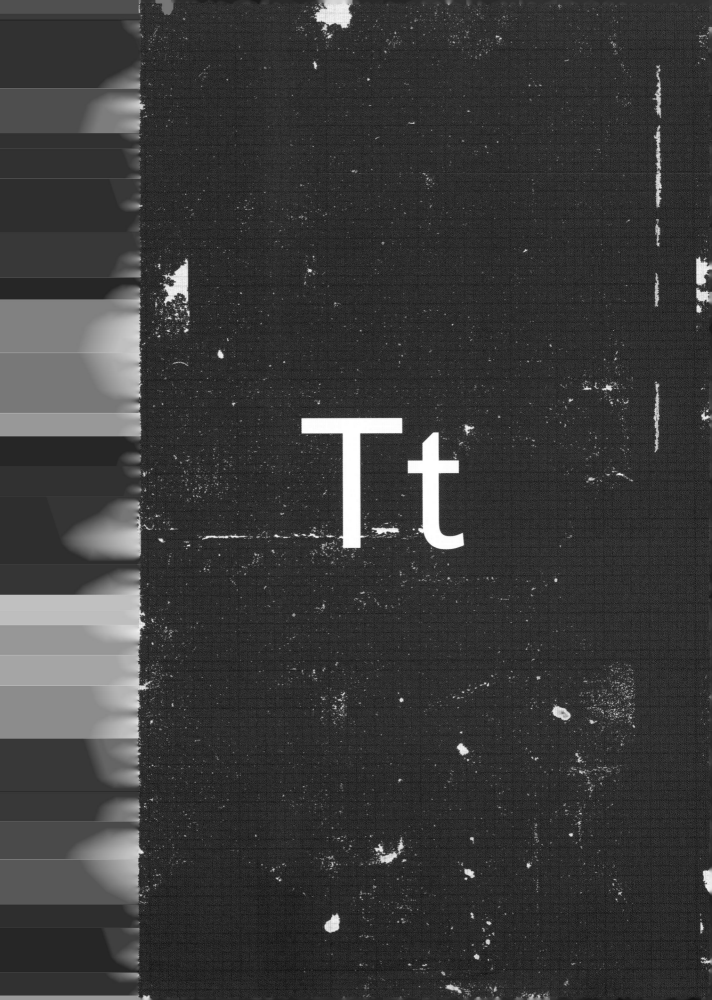

Tt

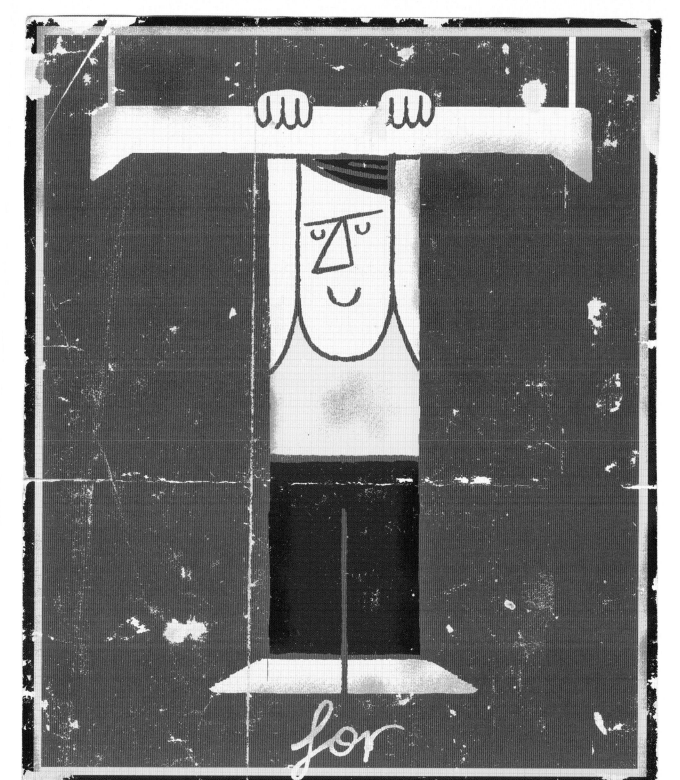

for
TRAPEZE

Uu

for

UNDERGROUND

Vv

for
VICIOUS

for

wave

Xx

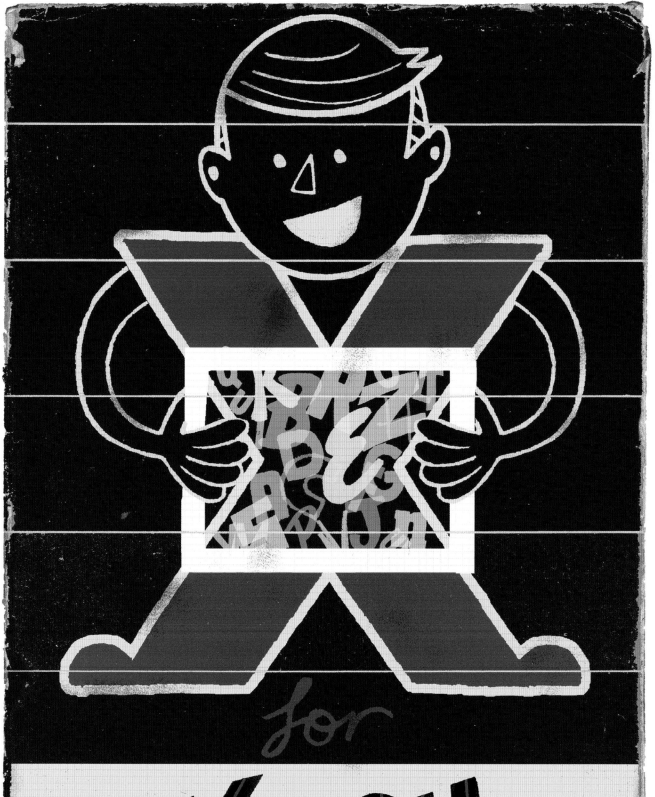

for

X-ray

Yy

for

Yoga

Zz

for

ZiP

Gadget

Galaxy

Gamble

Gape

Gargle

Gasp

Genie

Genetics

Giant

Gibbon

Gist

Gutter

Glass

Glue

Glow

Globe

Goldfish

Graffiti

Graphic

Greek

Greenery

Hang

Hula

H

Hurdle

X-ray

Xylophone

Yoga

Yield

ARTIST'S NOTE

When I started working on this alphabet, I had
no idea where it would take me and what it might
do for me. The recession had taken hold, it was the
middle of winter, and I had less work than usual
coming in. I needed a project to keep me occupied.

The idea for the alphabet came about partly
because of a book called ABC 3D, which I'd been
given for Christmas. I had already illustrated a
letter O for Owl, albeit in scratchy black-and-white.
It seemed a good idea to go back and begin with A.
Yes, A for Awesome seemed a good place to start.

My alphabet needed to be different from the many versions around, so I decided to pursue the challenge of fusing the object of the word with the shape of the letter. The series picked up interest as I posted each new letter online when I finished it. The Internet is an incredible promotional tool, and word soon spread via many design and illustration blogs. I thank each and every one of those bloggers for that encouragement, since, as a result, this alphabet series has transformed my career and led to some exciting commissions. A literary agent noticed my alphabet on one of the blogs, and because of that, you now have this book in front of you!

The inspiration for my work comes from mid-century design and illustration. My style has been described as being retro-modern. I use old books, postcards, and pieces of paper for the backgrounds. I will often buy an old book just to use its back cover!

With special thanks to my two Jeans: my agent, Jean Sagendorph, and my longtime friend and inspiration, Jean Pikett.

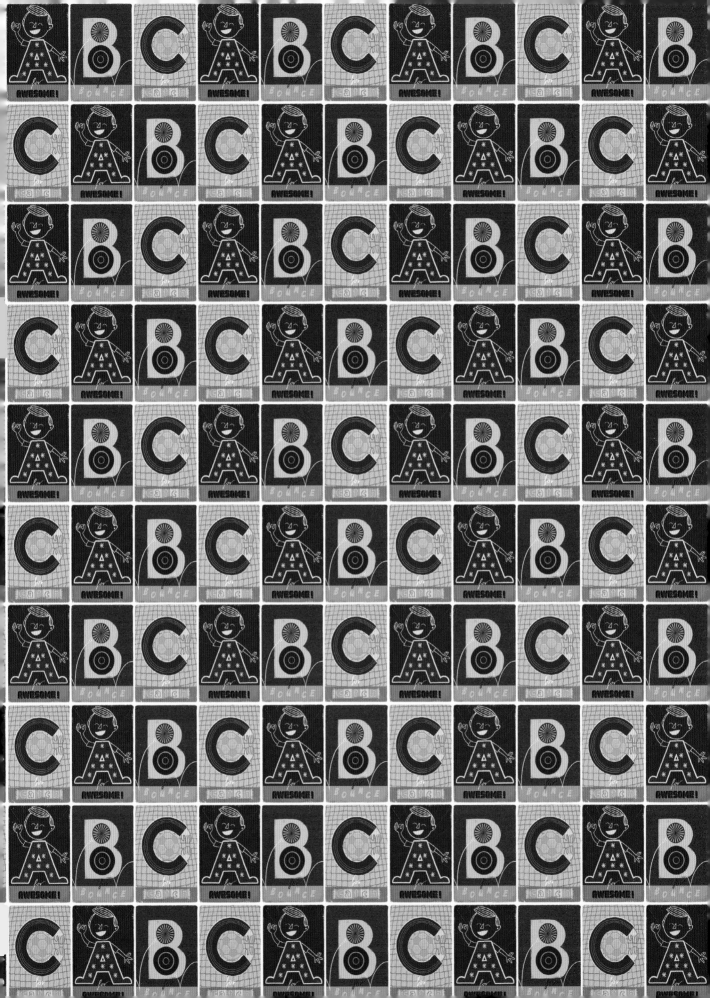